Cassie Kingston Mysteries

The Message in the Transom

❖

J.H. Sweet

A little mystery is good for the soul.

Cassie Kingston Mysteries

❖

The Message in the Transom
The Candlewick Inn Mystery
The Statue in Glen Park
The Painting of Swan Cove Island

❖

jhsweet.com

Contents

Chapter One
Heirloom Roses

Summer break was not even two days old, and Cassie Kingston already had half of her activities planned for the next two months. And if the last three summers were anything to go by, Cassie would be spending nearly every minute of her time with her best friend, Enilsa Santos.

The first of their summer plans involved something really grimy because they were going to help transplant several heirloom rosebushes and, therefore, would be digging in dirt.

A friend of Cassie's parents, a gardener named Mr. Zimmer, had arranged for them to help with this project. Cassie and Enilsa were thrilled, mainly because they were going to get paid for their work. They were each saving up for something special, and it wasn't always easy for ten-year-olds to find ways to earn spending money in a fairly small city. Actually, many people considered West Bend to be something between a town and a city based on its size. But either way, there just wasn't much in the way of odd jobs to earn money.

Cassie and Enilsa met two other project helpers, Roberta and Kyle Harrison, who were a year ahead of them in school, very early in the morning on the front lawn of *Ninety-Seven Burleson Avenue*. They had all walked to the house because Burleson Avenue wasn't far from any of their homes.

Roberta and Kyle were twins, and they were also excited to be able to earn a little extra money. Roberta was more talkative than her brother, who seemed somewhat shy, and she chatted enthusiastically with Cassie and Enilsa.

Mr. Zimmer met them about fifteen minutes later, with shovels and transplanting pots, to begin giving them their instructions. The gardener was a jovial man with a red face and bushy white hair. He led them around to one side of the house to show them the sixteen bushes that needed to be moved.

"Now these are not the kind of heirloom roses you can just order from a catalog," Mr. Zimmer began, pulling several pairs of gloves from his pockets. "These are very old, and they are the kind of rosebushes that get passed down to people from generation to generation."

The four helpers nodded their understanding, since Mr. Zimmer was obviously trying to impress upon them the need to be careful.

With a smile, the gardener continued. "I pruned them up last week to get them ready for the trip." He then proceeded to demonstrate with the first bush exactly how wide and how deep to dig to get the correct amount of roots.

After filling one of the transplanting pots with some of the loose dirt from the hole, Mr. Zimmer, with Enilsa's help, proceeded to carefully lift the first rosebush into its container. Then, Roberta and Enilsa filled the pot, carefully packing dirt around the roots of the bush, so it would be secure for its trip.

"We won't water 'til we plant because these babies are getting settled into their new homes right away," said Mr. Zimmer. "They are going to be planted in the Town Square. I already dug the holes."

As Cassie and Kyle began digging around two of the other bushes, Mr. Zimmer explained, "The city owns this old house, but it's going to be torn down. The estate is over four acres, and they are going to make it into a park."

Shaking his head slightly, Mr. Zimmer added, "The house was supposed to become the Town History Museum, but it needs a lot of repair, and the city doesn't have the funds. I guess a park will be much cheaper to build and easier to maintain."

Indicating the rear of the property, the gardener stated, "We're keeping as much of the landscaping as possible—the fruit trees, the wisteria, the flower beds—but the roses are too close to the house. Since they are so valuable, the city decided to move them to the Town Square. That'll be a good place for them, and a lot of people will be able to enjoy them there."

As all four of the helpers began digging in earnest, Mr. Zimmer told them that he needed to leave to check on another job, but that he would be back in about two hours. After getting four plastic cups out of his truck, the gardener came back for a moment and said, "I'll unlock the door of the house, so you can use the bathroom if you need to. They gave me the keys because I'm out here so much lately. It took me two whole days last week to prune the wisteria back from the fence and haul off the vines. It was so overgrown."

Mr. Zimmer obviously liked to visit and discuss his work. The helpers nodded politely as they dug. However, the gardener quickly decided that he really did need to be going. "Anyway," he said, "here are some cups if you want to go in to get water. Digging's hard work, especially in the summer, and you'll likely get pretty thirsty. Just remember to wipe your feet really good."

As they worked, Roberta visited with Cassie and Enilsa, while Kyle mainly kept silent. He seemed a quiet type and obviously preferred to keep his distance from the girls. His sister, however, had a very bubbly personality; and the effort of digging did nothing to hinder her chatter. Cassie and Enilsa listened politely as Roberta filled them in on which movie she and her brother had seen the week before, how many times they had gone to the community pool in the past month, the fact that she preferred violets to roses, and the exact words her elderly neighbors had uttered when departing for the grocery store at seven in the morning.

After touching on a few other fairly unimportant matters, Roberta told her new friends, "You know...I was supposed to be a Robert."

"What?" asked Cassie.

Nodding, Roberta went on. "Yep. The sonogram showed two boys. The doctors were, like, a hundred percent sure. So Mom and Dad had already picked out the names Kyle and Robert. Then I came out, and they had to think super-quick to come up with a girl's name."

Kyle finally said something at this point. "So they just took the easy route and sort of recycled the name they had already picked."

"Oh, that's interesting," said Enilsa. "I would have thought you were named after an aunt or grandmother, since Roberta is kind of an old-fashioned name."

"Or maybe an uncle," said Cassie, "kind of like making Henry into Henrietta, or Albert into Alberta."

"I'm named after an uncle," said Kyle.

Since the ice was now broken, Kyle joined in the pleasant conversation, and the friends had a lot of fun visiting while they worked.

Chapter Two
Stained Glass

An hour later, they had nearly finished their project. Since Roberta needed to use the bathroom, and they were all thirsty, they brushed off as much dirt as possible, retrieved the plastic cups, and headed up to the front porch of the house. Two sets of wind chimes hanging from the eaves by the steps tinkled pleasantly at them as they carefully wiped their feet on the doormat.

Inside, they were careful not to touch anything as they headed through the parlor into the dining room and kitchen. However, they did walk slowly to admire the antique furniture and rugs. Kyle was especially fascinated with the gigantic fireplace, having never seen one as large before.

After filling the cups with water from the kitchen tap, Roberta and Cassie looked for a downstairs bathroom, which was easy to find in the hall behind the dining room.

After using the facilities, Cassie and Roberta joined Enilsa and Kyle in the parlor. Admiring the charm of the old house and its furnishings, the group found themselves particularly drawn to a unique stained glass transom window above the double doors leading to the large living area of the house. In addition to a pretty and colorful glass design, the transom contained a three-lined message.

In this house
lies a treasure beyond measure ~
Harmony.

"It's like a little poem," said Roberta.

"Or a proverb," mused Cassie.

"You're right," replied Kyle, "because it's probably referring to family being in harmony, or maybe friends that visit—people getting along, good cheer, that kind of stuff."

The others agreed, and they all felt that the house was indeed very harmonious because the atmosphere was extremely peaceful and calm.

"The saying definitely fits," said Enilsa. Tilting her head slightly to one side, she added, "But the pattern seems a little odd."

Studying the glass, her friends could tell immediately what she was referring to. A scrolling pattern of bronze bells, blue and green ribbons, and golden curlicues surrounded the words of the message.

Enilsa was a very technical and scientific type of person, most of the time, and she always noticed things that seemed out of place. Of the two best friends, Cassie was much less of a serious, all-business type than Enilsa. However, Cassie was easily able to pick up on small details, and she too had noticed that something didn't seem quite right. "I see what you mean," she said. "The pattern doesn't really fit with the flower theme in the rest of the house."

However, at the moment, they couldn't spend any more time pondering, or admiring the contents of the house, because they really needed to be getting back outside to finish their job.

After exiting the house, they finished potting up the rosebushes in about thirty minutes. Mr. Zimmer arrived shortly after that to help them load the containers into the back of his pick-up truck.

Since the truck had a stretch cab with a large back seat, they were all able to ride with him to the Town Square, where they quickly set to work planting the heirloom roses.

While they worked, they talked about the house, and the landscaping, and the gigantic fireplace, and the unusual glass transom. Mr. Zimmer overheard part of their conversation, and he told them, "If you want to know more about that house, you could ask Mrs. Brinkley. She knows just about everything about the town, and she used to live on the other end of Burleson Avenue."

The helpers agreed this was a good suggestion, since they were very curious about the house and its history. So Mr. Zimmer gave them Mrs. Brinkley's address, which was within walking distance from the Town Square. "She loves visitors," he said, "so you can probably just stop by without even calling first."

Chapter Three
Mrs. Brinkley

When the rosebush transplanting was finished, Mr. Zimmer paid his helpers. But he didn't drive them to their homes as he had originally planned because they had decided to walk to Mrs. Brinkley's house to see if she was home. Though they were starting to get hungry, it was still about an hour before their normal lunchtime, so they thought they would have plenty of time.

They reached their destination on Ash Drive in less than ten minutes. Mrs. Brinkley was sitting in a rocker on her porch, and she called to them before they were even halfway up the walk to the house. "I baked cookies this morning!

Now how could I have known you were going to stop by?"

As they climbed the porch steps, Cassie and her friends wondered the same thing, since none of them had ever met Mrs. Brinkley before.

The white-haired woman ended her greeting with, "I must be psychic. I'm Roberta Brinkley, by the way."

"That's *my* name!" exclaimed Roberta. "I mean, my first name is Roberta." She had never met another Roberta before.

"It's a very pretty name," responded Mrs. Brinkley, "if I do say so myself."

As Enilsa, Kyle, and Cassie introduced themselves, Mrs. Brinkley nodded and said, "Have a seat, and some cookies." The oatmeal raisin cookies were still slightly warm, and they were wonderful.

The visitors were careful to use the napkins stacked next to the cookie platter.

"Oh, don't worry about the crumbs," exclaimed Mrs. Brinkley, when she noticed Kyle bending to retrieve a dropped raisin. "For goodness sakes! This is the porch! What good is a porch, if you can't drop a few crumbs on it?"

As the visitors smiled, Mrs. Brinkley added, "Now, what can I do for you this morning?"

Swallowing a cookie mouthful, Cassie replied, "We were wondering if you could tell us something about *Ninety-Seven Burleson Avenue?*"

Mrs. Brinkley looked sharply at Cassie, as if very surprised by the question, so Cassie went on to explain, "We were helping Mr. Zimmer transplant rosebushes from the house to the Town Square, and he suggested that we talk to you. It's such an interesting house. We had a peek inside, so we were just wondering if you could tell us something about it."

Mrs. Brinkley smiled and nodded. "Well, you came to the right place," she said. "I grew up down the street from the Lippincott Estate."

The visitors listened carefully as the woman went on. "Laura and David Lippincott lived at *Number Ninety-Seven* long after their parents passed on. Then David moved away. But Laura lived there until her dying day.

"Oh there's nothing to fret about," Mrs. Brinkley said, noting their concerned expressions at the mention of someone dying. "Laura outlived her brother and didn't pass on until the ripe old age of ninety-two. We should all be so lucky to live that long."

After a moment's pause, Mrs. Brinkley continued. "Laura Lippincott was a great friend of my mothers. I remember they used to play cards together a couple days a week. But she kept to herself mostly because she was rather shy. Neither she nor David ever had any children, and that's how the city ended up with the property. Since Laura didn't have an heir, she left the house and property, and everything else she owned, to the city."

Mrs. Brinkley sighed as she added, "Her request was for the city to use the house for a museum, since we don't have a Town History Museum. But I guess it's more cost-effective to just clear the property and put in a few benches and some playground equipment."

"Couldn't someone do some fundraising?" asked Enilsa.

"Restoring an old house like that, and keeping it up, can be very costly." Mrs. Brinkley shook her head. "I doubt enough money could be raised. And even though it's one of the oldest houses in town, it was never registered as an official *Historic Home*, so I don't think there's really enough interest in trying to save it."

Next, Mrs. Brinkley became very thoughtful as she further reminisced. "Come to think of it, David was a lot like his sister, as far as being shy and quiet, and keeping to himself. But I remember he used to collect coins. Once, when I went with Mother to have tea there—oh, I was just a girl—he showed me some of his collection."

Since Mrs. Brinkley had provided them with so much information, the visitors couldn't particularly think of anything else to ask her. So they soon bid her farewell and rose to leave.

"You are welcome to come by anytime for another visit," stated Mrs. Brinkley. "I usually make chocolate chip cookies on Tuesdays," she hinted, winking. Then she handed out two more cookies to each of her guests to take with them.

"Thank you," Cassie and Roberta said in unison.

Because their mouths were again full of oatmeal raisin cookie bites, Enilsa and Kyle just waved as they headed down the porch steps.

At the corner of Zahn and Mitchell, Cassie and Enilsa said goodbye to Kyle and Roberta. Before leaving, Roberta gave Enilsa her phone number, so they could all keep in touch. Even though Roberta was a year older than Cassie and Enilsa, she liked making as many new friends as possible.

Chapter Four
The Out-of-Place Staircase

After waving goodbye to the twins, Cassie and Enilsa headed to Cassie's house for lunch.

They washed up first, then had turkey sandwiches, corn chips, and apples. As they were cleaning up afterwards, Enilsa, who had been doing some pondering, said, "You know, we could get my camera and take a few pictures of the house before it gets torn down. Then we would have some sort of a record of its existence."

"That's a great idea!" exclaimed Cassie.

"Then I'll take pictures of the park too when it's finished," mused Enilsa, "so we'll have like a before and after of Lippincott Park. I assume the city will name the park after the person who donated the property."

"I would hope so," said Cassie.

Cassie's mother worked afternoons at an insurance agency, so Cassie made a quick call to her mother's work to let her know what she and Enilsa were planning for the afternoon. Then the two headed for Enilsa's house, just two blocks away, to pick up her camera and tell her mom what they were doing.

When they again reached *Ninety-Seven Burleson Avenue*, they found Mr. Zimmer putting netting over several peach trees. "It keeps the birds from eating the fruit," he stated, climbing down from the ladder.

Mr. Zimmer thought Enilsa's idea of photographing the house was an excellent one, and he suggested that they take pictures inside too. Cassie and Enilsa were thrilled at the prospect of getting to see the inside of the home again. The gardener unlocked the door for them, as he said, "We should enjoy the house while we can, since it will be gone soon." Then he went back to his peach-tree task.

After taking a few shots of the outside of the house from various positions on the lawns and front walk, the two stepped inside, being careful to wipe their feet on the doormat.

Enilsa took pictures of the downstairs rooms first. As they passed from the parlor into the living room, Cassie said, "We forgot to ask Mrs. Brinkley about the stained glass."

Nodding as she snapped a picture of the transom, Enilsa said, "We could visit her again. She did invite us."

"Yes," agreed Cassie. "And we should make sure to go on a Tuesday." (Chocolate chip cookies were Cassie's favorite of all cookies.)

After taking pictures of every room downstairs, including the two bathrooms, the pair headed up the staircase in the living room. There was another large staircase in a wide hall at the rear of the house, but the two decided to begin their exploration of the second floor in the front of the home. The house was only two stories, but it also had an attic and a basement, which Enilsa decided they should photograph last, in case she should run out of memory-card space on her camera.

Enilsa carefully took one picture of each room upstairs. While exploring, they found a small stair leading up to the attic. However, they decided not to go up just yet because they were suddenly very confused about something. Having roamed every inch of the second floor, twice, they were unable to find the second large staircase, which they had expected would lead them down into the wide hall on the first floor at the rear of the house.

"We can look in the attic later," said Cassie, excitedly. "Let's go back down and see where that other staircase leads."

Enilsa immediately agreed, and the two sped back down the front stairs and rushed through the living area to reach the back hall.

The wide hall contained several benches and chairs, along with two short stone columns upon which sat ornate vases. And the walls were filled with paintings, mainly of the landscape type.

"This must be a gallery," said Cassie, with Enilsa nodding.

Facing the staircase, which was every bit as wide and seemed to have about the same number of steps as the front stairs, the two looked up at the solid double doors staring back at them from the top of the landing. The doors were shut, so there was no way to tell what lay beyond them.

The house suddenly seemed even quieter than before, as the two slowly ascended the stairs. Both Enilsa and Cassie sensed something unusual, even aside from their curiosity as to where the mysterious staircase might lead them.

When they reached the landing, they both took a deep breath as Cassie took hold of both doorknobs, turned, and pulled open the doors.

The pair immediately squinted and shielded their eyes as sunlight flooded into the house. Then they stepped out onto a tee-tiny balcony barely two feet deep and only as wide as the double doors. Looking out, they could see Mr. Zimmer at the rear of the property, weeding an iris bed. Just below them, the edge of the back patio met an old vegetable garden plot, which had not been planted so far this year, since Laura Lippincott had passed away during the winter.

Confused as to why such a large staircase would lead to such a tiny balcony, Enilsa and Cassie decided to forgo taking pictures of the attic and basement, in lieu of asking Mr. Zimmer what he knew about the odd staircase. Since the back door was locked with a kind of lock that required a key to open it from the inside, they headed out the front door and around the house to talk to the gardener.

"Hmmm..." said Mr. Zimmer, when they described the stair and balcony to him. Staring at the back of the house, and specifically at the balcony in question, he added, "That *is* odd. I don't know why anyone would have built such a large staircase just to reach a tiny balcony that is even too tiny to sit out on." Shaking his head, he added, "I'm stumped. You might need to make another trip to Mrs. Brinkley's, to ask her about it."

Cassie and Enilsa agreed. However, they also both suddenly realized that they needed to be getting home in a hurry because they were supposed to meet several of their friends in the late afternoon for a bake-sale fundraiser.

As they said goodbye to Mr. Zimmer, he told them, "If you find out about that staircase, let me know, because I'm pretty curious about it too."

The girls agreed as they sped off.

After rushing to their separate homes, the two gathered up their previously baked goodies and hurried to meet four of their friends outside the supermarket, which was within walking distance from their homes.

Cassie and Enilsa were both in the choir at school, and the fundraiser was going to help pay for their fall trip. The local grocery store often let kids set up and sell things for fundraisers. And one of the area banks was good about letting them hold carwashes in the parking lot on weekends.

Although the fundraiser was fun, the whole time they were selling fudge, cupcakes, muffins, and cookies, Enilsa and Cassie couldn't stop thinking about the Lippincott House, and particularly, the out-of-place staircase.

Chapter Five
Paint and Pigs

Unfortunately, Enilsa and Cassie weren't going to be able to visit Mrs. Brinkley the next morning because they had volunteered to help with a town project. About twenty-five people met in the Town Square very early in order to repaint the old gazebo. The volunteers included a mix of both grown-ups and kids, and the group was planning to have a cook-out afterwards. A man who owned a local barbeque restaurant had already set up and fired up his grill by the time Cassie and Enilsa arrived.

Mrs. Patterson, who owned the local paint store, had also come early. And Enilsa and Cassie were thrilled to see Kyle and Roberta helping to unload gallon paint buckets from Mrs. Patterson's van. The twins were also happy to see their new friends.

The mayor, Mr. Barnard, arrived just as the group was getting started. He was planning to help too. Mr. Barnard had brought his two potbellied pigs, Napoleon and Caesar, with him on leashes. He tied the leashes to a tree limb, so his pets could enjoy the shade, and he set out a large pan of water for them.

Next, using paint scrapers and block sanders to remove as much of the old paint as possible, the group set to work on the gazebo. A local contractor was planning to have his employees replace the roof at a later time, so today was just for painting.

Cassie and Enilsa worked next to Roberta and Kyle. While they scraped and sanded, they talked about the house on Burleson Avenue, and Cassie and Enilsa shared the details of their second visit with the twins.

Roberta and Kyle were equally puzzled about the staircase, and they too thought it would be a good idea to revisit Mrs. Brinkley.

"I can't believe you found something even stranger than that transom window," said Roberta.

"Many older houses are very strange," said Kyle. "I think it has to do with what was going on in the world when they were built."

"Like when people built fall-out shelters during wartimes," Enilsa said.

Kyle nodded. "Exactly."

"They used to plant Victory Gardens during wartime too," said Roberta. "And some people still keep up those old city gardens, since they are a big part of our history."

"But that staircase is just so odd," stated Cassie, as she attacked a stubborn patch of old paint with her sanding block. Breathing a little hard, she added, "It's a lot more out of place than a stained glass transom that doesn't match flowery furniture and drapes. I mean, the staircase doesn't really have any purpose." Cassie was a little frustrated with herself because she was usually able to figure things like this out fairly easily.

"Unless…" began Roberta.

When she didn't go on, Cassie asked, "What?"

Laughing a little, Roberta said, "I was just thinking of something like a *Romeo and Juliet* balcony—for someone to stand out on to listen to a serenade, or to gaze at the moon."

"That's pretty far-fetched," said Enilsa. "Someone could just build a balcony off of a bedroom for that. They wouldn't need a gigantic separate staircase."

"I know," said Roberta. "The thought just popped into my head. I knew it wasn't right."

"It's good to brainstorm," said Cassie. "That's how people come up with some of their best ideas."

An elderly gentleman named Mr. Duncan was working near them, and he had overheard part of their conversation. "Are you talking about Laura Lippincott's place?" he asked.

"Yes!" responded Cassie. Hopeful that Mr. Duncan would be able to shed some light on this mystery, she hurriedly explained, "We had chance to see inside the house, and we were wondering about the back staircase. It seems odd for a large staircase to lead only to a small balcony."

"The house was once much larger," responded Mr. Duncan. "During an earthquake—oh, about forty-five years ago now—the back wing of the Lippincott house broke off and fell right into a huge crack."

"How terrible!" exclaimed Roberta.

Mr. Duncan nodded. "About half of West Bend was a pretty big mess. And everything in that part of the Lippincott house was completely smashed and destroyed. I think the back wing had four bedrooms upstairs. The downstairs part held a library, a second kitchen, and a small guest quarters.

"David and Laura were both gone at the time of the quake," Mr. Duncan went on. "A family friend who was looking after the house took it upon himself to get his uncle, who had a bulldozer, to fill in over the rubble and smooth everything over. It was a good judgment call because it wouldn't have been safe to leave it exposed like that, with all of the splintered wood, nails, sharp shingles, and other debris."

Cassie and her friends listened intently as Mr. Duncan continued. "When they got home, Laura and David were frantic because something extremely valuable had been stored in that part of the house. Sadly, nothing could be done. Whatever it was probably got destroyed anyway, or was at least seriously damaged. They kept saying that they had lost something terribly valuable. But because neither of them would ever say what it was that was lost, a lot of people didn't believe them.

"A couple of weeks later," added Mr. Duncan, "they stopped talking about it. And other people stopped mentioning it to them, either because they didn't want to bring up painful memories for the two, or, like I said, they didn't believe them to start with."

After a pause, Mr. Duncan mused, "I think they probably did lose something valuable. But what is valuable to one person may not be to another."

"I imagine it was incredibly traumatic to lose that much of their house and belongings all at one time," said Kyle, "whether or not specific items were worth very much, moneywise."

"Do you know anything about the stained glass transom in the parlor?" Cassie suddenly remembered to ask.

Mr. Duncan shook his head as he answered. "Most of the exterior windows were broken during the earthquake, but I don't know anything about the interior glass.

"However…" he added, thoughtfully, "you might talk to Wanda Sloan at West Bend Glass Works. She'd remember if they made any stained glass for that house around that time."

Their conversation was suddenly interrupted by a tremendous ruckus on the opposite side of the gazebo. The group on that side had finished sanding and had started painting. Unfortunately, they hadn't been able to get very far because Mayor Barnard's potbellied pigs had gotten loose from their tree and had just upset and stepped in three gallons of paint. Then, Napoleon and Caesar had scampered all over the gazebo steps and platform to deposit as many painted hoof-prints as possible.

Several people, including the mayor, chased after the paint-covered pigs, while many others couldn't stop laughing.

About five minutes later, red-faced, and with a pig under each arm, Mr. Barnard apologized to everyone for the mishap. But most people didn't care because they were having so much fun. And no real harm was done because they had to paint the gazebo anyway. Nevertheless, the mayor's wife shortly carted Caesar and Napoleon off to home. Since the two couldn't behave themselves, they weren't going to be allowed to stay for the rest of the painting, or the barbeque.

Two hours later, when the painting was finished, many people spread out blankets in the grass surrounding the gazebo. Cassie, Enilsa, Kyle, and Roberta all sat together to enjoy their hot dogs, hamburgers, potato salad, and sodas.

Kyle seemed more comfortable now in talking to Enilsa and Cassie. When he finally managed to squeeze a few words in amongst his sister's chatter, he told them, "The message in the transom makes more sense now, if the

Lippincotts owned a treasure of some sort. I think we should talk to Mr. Zimmer again. Maybe he knows someone who could help dig up the buried part of house. Then we might be able to find the valuable item that was lost."

"A project like that would probably cost a lot of money," said Enilsa, who was always one to look at the practical side of things.

"Not if someone has the right equipment and is willing to donate their time," argued Kyle.

Cassie and Roberta agreed with Kyle.

"If we explain why we think it should be dug up," said Cassie, "someone might be willing to help." Always an optimist, she added hopefully, "Maybe we'll find a real treasure. And if we find something really valuable, that would be a good way to fund the house restoration and museum project, as Laura Lippincott wished. Then the city wouldn't need to tear the house down."

The others agreed that the idea was a good one. However, Enilsa, always cautious and slightly skeptical, said, "If whatever was lost was tremendously valuable, why didn't Laura Lippincott ever dig it up herself?"

"Maybe she never had extra money to hire anyone to do it," said Roberta.

"And digging equipment like bulldozers might not have been easily obtained," said Kyle. "They probably couldn't spare another one soon after the earthquake, since the equipment would have been needed for repairs and new construction," he further explained. "Then, renting one later might have been too expensive for her to manage."

Since his explanation sounded plausible, Enilsa didn't raise any other questions. Plus, she couldn't deny that the prospect of looking for a buried treasure was incredibly exciting, even if it meant trying to get a bulldozer and operator to help for free.

Chapter Six
The Excavation

Mr. Zimmer was still working at the house the next morning when the hopeful treasure hunters arrived. Pruning a clump of silver sage bushes, he was happy to see the visitors.

Cassie hurriedly explained what they had learned from Mr. Duncan, to which Mr. Zimmer replied, "I remember that earthquake, but I didn't live here at the time, so I didn't know this house lost a wing." Looking closely at the structure, he added, "Come to think of it, those shingles under the balcony don't match perfectly with the rest of the back of the house. They are a little darker. If I had looked more closely, I would have been able to tell that that section had been repaired or replaced."

Next, Kyle explained that they were hopeful someone with a bulldozer might be able to do a little digging in the area of the buried wing, so they could look for whatever the Lippincotts lost that might have been valuable.

Mr. Zimmer took off his cap to scratch his head. Evidently deep in thought, he scrunched up his face for a few moments before he replied. "Well…" he began. "Let's see…tomorrow's Friday…and they are going to have a bulldozer out here next week anyway when they start tearing down the house. I could talk to the contractor to see if they can get it out here sooner."

The four friends got very excited, as the gardener added, "I can't see any harm in it. They have to excavate some anyway to pour the slab for the park pavilion. And from what I remember of the design for the park, the pavilion is going to be about where the garden plot is now. So that should be the right spot. They might as well dig a little deeper, since they already have the equipment."

Kyle was smiling broadly, since his idea had obviously been a good one, while the girls were fairly bouncing up and down at the thought of possibly finding a buried treasure.

However, noting their very obvious enthusiasm, Mr. Zimmer decided to caution them. "You should keep in mind that even if I can get someone out here to dig, they won't be able to spend a lot of time on the project. I would think maybe only about half a day. Then, there's the issue of the stuff being under the ground for so long, with the rain, temperature changes, and other factors. What's down there might be pretty rotted away by now."

The four nodded their understanding, but were still hopeful that something valuable might be uncovered during the excavation.

Since Mr. Zimmer really needed to get back to pruning the sage bushes, he said, "If you can come by again tomorrow morning, around eight, I should be able to let you know if and when the bulldozer can be arranged."

They agreed, thanking Mr. Zimmer, as they said goodbye and left him to his work.

The next morning, Mr. Zimmer had already managed to make the arrangements, and a bright yellow bulldozer greeted the group as they arrived.

A man was just climbing down from the dozer as they walked up, and Mr. Zimmer introduced him as Mr. Haupt. Mr. Haupt gave each of them a hardhat to wear while they watched him work and told them how far back to stand from the digging. Then he hopped back up to the seat of the bulldozer and started the engine.

Since the ground was fairly soft in the area of the garden, the digging progressed rather quickly. In less than an hour, a large hole was already forming. Instead of one big pile, Mr. Haupt made several smaller piles of debris around the edge of the hole, so the dirt and rubble would be easier to sort through.

A short while later, when Mr. Haupt had excavated a fairly good-sized chunk of the fallen house wing, he stopped the bulldozer. Climbing down, he gave each of them a pair of work gloves. Then, he and Mr. Zimmer supervised their rooting through the piles of rubble.

"Watch for glass and other sharp things," warned Mr. Haupt. "And don't walk on any loose boards because nobody wants to step on a nail and end up having to go to the clinic for a tetanus shot."

Mr. Zimmer was nodding. "I had to get one last year, and it felt like I had a golf ball in my arm for about three weeks. I can't stand shots."

They were careful, and no one stepped on any nails. However, unfortunately, just as Mr. Zimmer had predicted, the remains of the wing of the house, and its contents, were badly deteriorated. As they worked to pull apart and sift through the rubble piles, they found mostly splintered and rotted wood.

Cassie and Enilsa found the smashed remains of a dresser with an attached mirror, but the contents of the drawers were not recognizable as anything other than dusty soot. Roberta and Kyle found pieces of a couple of doors, with their glass knobs still attached, and a rusty old sewing machine. Unfortunately, their search yielded nothing more valuable.

Observing their progress, Mr. Haupt told them, "Even if what you are looking for survived, if it is fairly small, you might never find it."

Mr. Zimmer agreed. "It would be like looking for a needle in a haystack," he said. "And even if we did come across it, we might not recognize it, covered with dirt." Though these were wise words, the hopeful searchers weren't ready to give up yet.

However, after an hour more of digging through dirt and debris, they finally had to admit defeat and end their search.

Disappointed, Cassie told her friends, "I was just hoping that if David lost some of his valuable coins, or if it was a piece of jewelry or something, that we might find it in a box. But it doesn't look like any boxes at all survived being buried."

Roberta sighed. "Everything's too far gone," she said sadly.

"But it was a really good idea," said Enilsa, directing her comment toward Kyle, who looked very disappointed (and felt slightly foolish) about having suggested the excavation.

"It was a good idea," agreed Mr. Zimmer. "We just came up empty handed."

"I'm going to park the dozer under that pecan tree for the weekend," Mr. Haupt told Mr. Zimmer. "Will it be out of your way there?"

"Oh, yes," responded Mr. Zimmer. "That will be fine."

As they thanked him for his help, Mr. Haupt collected the gloves and hardhats from the temporary workers and said goodbye to them before climbing back up to the bulldozer to move it. "I'm sorry we didn't find what you were looking for," he called to them.

They waved to Mr. Haupt and said goodbye to Mr. Zimmer who was heading toward the rear of the property to get back to work. Then, with shoulders slumped, Enilsa, Kyle, Cassie, and Roberta silently made their way around to the front of the house.

Chapter Seven
Laura's Diaries

Although they were disappointed by the fruitless excavation, they were not completely out of hope, because Cassie suddenly remembered something. "We haven't asked about the transom yet," she said.

"That's right," said Kyle. "We were supposed to talk to Wanda Sloan at West Bend Glass Works."

Though it was nearly lunchtime, the friends hurried downtown together to the glass store. When they asked for Wanda Sloan, an elderly woman came out of the back to talk to them. "Yes. I remember that transom window very well," she said. "We made it about six months after the quake. It was a special order. Laura had it drawn out on paper, exactly how she wanted it."

"But do you know if the saying refers to anything in particular?" asked Cassie.

"Or if the design means anything?" added Enilsa.

Mrs. Sloan shook her head. "I just thought Laura was redecorating. I'm afraid I didn't think much about it, and I never asked. We were so busy that year."

Cassie nodded. "Well…thank you," she said.

The others also thanked Mrs. Sloan, and Enilsa picked up one of the glass works' business cards because she liked to collect business cards.

After leaving the shop, the friends decided to have lunch together at the Dairy Queen.

Cassie was still puzzling over the transom the whole time they were eating. A short while later, as they were ordering ice cream, a brainstorm finally hit her, and she told her friends, "The transom was made *after* the earthquake."

"Yes," said Enilsa, in a manner that clearly meant she was thinking, *We already know that.*

With her friends looking questioningly at her, Cassie explained, "If the message about treasure and harmony isn't meant to refer to the harmony of family or friends, then maybe she found what she thought she lost."

"Oh, I see," said Roberta. "The message in the glass must refer to the contents of the house after the quake, since that was when the glass was made."

Nodding, Kyle added, "Mr. Duncan did say that Laura and David dropped the issue of losing something valuable after a couple of weeks."

"They probably found whatever it was!" said Enilsa.

"And maybe it's still there," said Cassie, "unless they sold it later."

"I doubt they would have sold something that important to them," said Roberta, breathlessly.

They took their ice cream cones with them in order to walk back to the Lippincott house as quickly as possible. Fortunately, Mr. Zimmer was still there. After explaining that they hoped to look for the possible treasure inside the house, Mr. Zimmer said, "Well, I can't see any harm in that." As he unlocked the door for them, he added, "They're moving out the furniture on Monday morning, so it's now or never if you want to look for anything. I think they are donating most of it to the thrift shop. Except the books; those will go to the library."

They began their search downstairs and carefully looked in all drawers and cupboards, and under sofa cushions. They also searched behind books on bookshelves and examined Laura Lippincott's other belongings, while being extremely careful to handle all delicate items gently and put things back in their places.

Finding nothing that seemed overly valuable downstairs, they moved up to the second floor to continue their search.

In one of the bedrooms, they found a set of eleven thick diaries, all bound in dark green leather, sitting on a bookshelf beside the bed.

"This must have been Laura's bedroom," said Cassie, as she carefully flipped the pages of the first diary.

"Wow!" exclaimed Roberta, opening one of the later volumes. "She kept a diary nearly her whole life."

Enilsa was examining another of the books, and she said, "But I wonder if it's okay to look in someone else's diaries."

"She doesn't have any family that we can ask," said Kyle, "and we are trying to do something helpful."

"If we find anything too personal, we can stop reading," suggested Cassie.

"They don't have locks," said Roberta, hopefully, as if finding a diary without a lock meant that the owner was okay with someone reading it.

Though her conscience was bothering her, Enilsa was trying to talk herself into it. "Since she's passed on," she said, "and we're trying to do something good…it's probably okay."

The others agreed. They also agreed to look at the entries around the time of the earthquake first, because that would be a good place to start.

After about five minutes of searching the volumes for the correct year and entries, Roberta found what they were looking for. "You were right!" she said. "They found it!" However, shaking her head slightly in confusion, she added, "But the way Laura words it here is just as mysterious as the message in the transom." Roberta then proceeded to read the diary entry aloud to her friends.

"We found it! It wasn't in the East Wing after all. David was so happy. He's the only one who knows the secret, aside from me. Clue for the future (in case I forget when I grow old and grey): The treasure is stored in Green in Blue in Red."

As they pondered the words, no one said anything for a few moments. Then Kyle remembered, "One of the photo albums in the parlor has a red cover."

"There's also a red lacquer cabinet in the dining room," said Cassie. "I noticed it particularly because antique lacquer cabinets are pretty valuable. My mom has wanted one for years."

"The reproductions cost less," said Enilsa, in a businesslike manner. "And the one downstairs is in such good shape, it's probably a reproduction. But you're right," she added, "the really old ones that are true antiques are usually very expensive."

They decided to look in the lacquer cabinet first, before checking out the photo album.

Cassie held her breath as she opened the cabinet doors. Since there was no squeak of the hinges, and the inside actually smelled a little bit like cedar, instead of musty or dusty old wood, the group decided that this probably was a newer cabinet, as opposed to a really old one. But that hardly mattered at this point, because they found exactly what they were looking for—a small green trunk, wrapped tightly in a blue blanket. "*Green in Blue in Red*,'" breathed Cassie.

The girls allowed Kyle, who seemed to want to very badly, to use his muscles to hoist the trunk out of the lacquer cabinet. He carefully set it onto the dining room rug; then he stepped back.

For some reason Cassie was reluctant to open the trunk. Her stomach fluttering wildly, she suddenly felt very flushed. Roberta and Enilsa were waiting for her to open it, so that she could have the first peek inside.

"You figured out most of the clues and pieced it all together," Enilsa told her best friend, "so you should have the first look."

Roberta and Kyle agreed.

But Cassie was just too nervous, and her hands were now sweating. "Please," she said, "just open it."

Kneeling, Roberta and Enilsa together did as Cassie asked and lifted the lid.

The trunk was filled with a wonderful assortment of childhood mementos including a toy fire truck, a set of wooden building blocks, a baseball and glove, a jack-in-the-box, and a doll wrapped in a small quilt.

Kyle lifted two picture storybooks out of the bottom to see if anything small lay beneath them. Having seen the baseball, his mind was now full of baseball cards, because he collected them; and he was thinking that the treasure might be something along the lines of valuable autographed baseball cards.

Under the doll wrapped in the quilt, Enilsa found a small box of coins that were individually sleeved.

The group was thrilled.

"This is probably it," breathed Cassie. "These coins might be valuable."

"We could ask the man at the coin shop," suggested Kyle.

Looking at her watch, Cassie said, "It's probably too late today."

"I wouldn't feel right about taking these with us," said Enilsa, "since they are not ours."

"And especially because they might be valuable," added Roberta.

"You're right," said Cassie. "We shouldn't take a chance on something happening to them."

"We could just leave them in the trunk," said Kyle, "and ask the man at the coin shop if he can come here tomorrow to look at them."

"Good idea," said Enilsa. Roberta and Cassie agreed.

After carefully repacking the trunk and placing it back into the lacquer cabinet, they locked up the house and went to tell Mr. Zimmer what they had found.

"Yes," said the gardener, "I'll be here again tomorrow, for most of the day, so I can unlock the house for you."

Even though the morning digging venture had been somewhat disappointing, the afternoon had turned out perfectly, and the four friends went home feeling excited and hopeful.

Chapter Eight
The Expert

The next morning, at eight forty-five, the friends met in front of the coin shop, which wasn't due to open until nine.

They were somewhat restless as they waited.

"I was thinking last night," began Roberta, "if the coins are really valuable, maybe they can sell for enough to restore the house. Then the city can make a museum, as Laura Lippincott wished."

"They would have to bring an awful lot of money for that to be possible," said Kyle.

"I would hate to speculate too much," said Cassie, "because we might end up disappointed."

Promptly at nine o'clock, the coin-shop owner, Mr. Wilson, arrived. "This is what I live for," he said happily, when they explained their request to him. "I love field trips to value coins."

Whistling, Mr. Wilson immediately closed up his shop, placing a sign on the door indicating he would, *Be back in an hour.*

Enilsa almost told Mr. Wilson that he hadn't put the time he was leaving on the sign, but she stopped herself, realizing that he probably did this a lot and didn't want people to know exactly when he was supposed to return, in case he wanted to take his time.

Mr. Wilson rode a moped scooter to work. However, since they couldn't all ride on one moped, he walked with them to *Ninety-Seven Burleson Avenue.* With a spring in his step, he chatted with them about the weather, the latest stamp and coin show he had been to, and about the newly painted town gazebo.

Mr. Zimmer was already there when they arrived, and he let them into the house right away.

Kyle again lifted the trunk from the red cabinet, and they took out the fire truck and quilt-wrapped doll to reach the coin box underneath them.

Mr. Wilson sat at the dining table to open the box and spread the coins out before him. He then pulled a jeweler's eyepiece from his pocket and immediately began studying one of the larger coins.

After examining each of the coins carefully, the expert stowed his eyepiece back into his pocket and said, "Two of these are valuable. Unfortunately," he added, "I think you are going to be disappointed because the whole lot is not worth more than three to four hundred dollars in total."

He was right; they were very disappointed. When no one said anything for nearly a minute, Mr. Wilson said, "I'm sorry. I know you were hoping they would be worth far more." Rising, and pointing to two of the coins on the table, he added, "These are the ones that will bring the most if sold." After a sigh, he said, "Well, I need to be getting back to the shop."

As they were seeing him to the front door, Mr. Wilson paused for a moment. "I have a suggestion for you," he said. "You might try to find out what those antique toys are worth. Some collectors are willing to pay a lot for old fire trucks and jack-in-the-boxes. Old quilts are sometimes worth a lot too," he added as he stepped out onto the front porch. "Well, goodbye. And good luck."

The friends were rather crestfallen, as they headed back to the dining room to repack the trunk.

However, as Cassie was wrapping the quilt more tightly around the doll, she suddenly noticed something. Moving the bundle to the table, she opened the quilt and carefully picked up the doll.

Laura had evidently taken very good care of her dolly, whose blond curls were untangled, clean, and bright. Also, the blue and green ribbons adorning the doll's dress weren't even wrinkled or crushed at all.

Roberta and Enilsa were also looking at the doll, while Kyle packed up the building blocks and fire truck.

"Oh my gosh!" said Cassie, as it finally dawned on her.

And both at the same time, Roberta and Enilsa exclaimed, "I know!"

Chapter Nine
Melody, Lyric, and Harmony

"She patterned the transom after her doll!" said Cassie, as Kyle joined them at the table, anxious to see what all the fuss was about.

The ribbons on the doll's dress were a perfect match to the scrolling ribbons surrounding the words on the transom. Upon lifting the hem of the dress, they found tiny bells sewn into the lace of the petticoats that were identical to those decorating the stained glass. The blond curlicues on the transom also now made sense because they very much resembled the doll's curly hair.

"So, is the doll a valuable antique?" asked Kyle.

"It looks too nice to be very old," said Enilsa. "But maybe Laura Lippincott just took really good care of it."

"Does this mean she named her doll, Harmony?" asked Roberta. "That would be a pretty name for a doll."

"Or maybe Harmony is a brand name of dolls," suggested Kyle.

"We could look online for that information," said Cassie.

The others agreed this was a good idea.

"My house is closest," said Cassie, carefully wrapping the doll back in the quilt and placing it into the trunk.

Kyle then carefully lifted the trunk back into the lacquer cabinet.

They left quickly, locking the door behind them. Then they sped around to the rear of the property to give Mr. Zimmer the key and an update. "So you think you found it," said Mr. Zimmer, smiling. "And it's a doll?"

"We think so," said Cassie. "But we're going to look things up to make sure, and we'd like to come back later, if that's okay."

"Sure," said Mr. Zimmer. "I'm kind of getting use to having you four around. But I'm going to my sister's house for lunch later, so I'll be gone from twelve to one."

They waved to Mr. Zimmer as they raced off to Cassie's house.

Unfortunately, when they looked up antique dolls online, they were unable to find out anything related to the word Harmony. The main problem was that too much information came up every time they searched. It didn't seem to matter if they eliminated words or added words to their search, there were just kazillions of sites devoted to antique dolls; and they never found a reference to Harmony because things about music and various charitable organizations kept coming up when they added the word Harmony to the search.

"This is just way too much information to wade through," said Enilsa. "And if they are going to start tearing down the house sometime next week, we might not find out anything useful until it's too late."

"What about trying to find a doll expert?" suggested Kyle. "We were able to find a coin expert, so maybe we could find one for dolls."

"That would be one way to do it," said Cassie, "but why don't we go to the library first? They probably have books on antique dolls. And that might be easier than wading through all of the massive stuff online."

"Good idea," said Enilsa.

However, since it was getting on lunch time, they hurriedly made up bologna sandwiches, with glasses of milk alongside. They also grabbed handfuls of grapes to take with them on the walk to the library, which was located near the Town Square.

The library had eight books on antique dolls. The friends sat at a table together, and each of them took one of the books from the stack to begin looking.

In the back of the second book she picked from the stack, Cassie actually found the word Harmony in the index.

"I found something," she said quietly, as she flipped the pages. And her eyes grew very round as she began to read.

Kyle, looking over her shoulder, nearly choked upon reaching the second paragraph.

Seeing her brother's reaction, Roberta got up and moved around to look over Cassie's shoulder too. Enilsa quickly followed.

With all of them straining to see the information, Cassie, in whispers, told her friends, "The doll is part of a trio of dolls, made as a set, but with each being truly one-of-a-kind. Melody, Lyric, and Harmony—a brunette, a redhead, and a blond.

Though black and white, the old photograph at the bottom of the page clearly showed Laura Lippincott's doll sitting next to her two sisters. There could be no mistake.

"They were made by a famous doll maker named Monterrey Brigita," Cassie continued. "He lived in New York City. Mr. Brigita only made about five dolls a year, but they were considered to be some of the finest dolls in the world."

"And they are very valuable," added Kyle, which is exactly what he had read in the second paragraph.

Cassie checked out the book so that they could take it with them, and they hurriedly left the library to return to the Lippincott Estate.

"I wonder how Miss Lippincott ended up with one of them," said Roberta, as they were walking.

The others couldn't come up with any good guesses, but Enilsa suddenly thought, "Maybe her diaries would explain that."

"Good idea," said Kyle, admiringly.

For some reason, Enilsa blushed, and her stomach jumped, when he said this. She looked away quickly, not really understanding her reaction. Since she had been feeling so comfortable around Kyle, it was weird that she could suddenly feel so unsettled just by the tone of his voice when he complimented her.

Mr. Zimmer was just pulling up in his truck from his luncheon when they arrived at the house.

Cassie and Roberta took turns excitedly telling Mr. Zimmer about the doll.

"Well, well, well," he said, looking at the picture in the book. "So you solved a pretty big mystery," he added.

"And if the doll is super-duper valuable," said Roberta, "maybe it would be enough to save this house."

"We were hoping," Cassie explained, "that whatever the treasure turned out to be, it would be enough to help fund restoration of the house and creation of the Town History Museum."

"But could a doll really be worth that much?" said Mr. Zimmer.

"We hope so," said Cassie. Then she asked Mr. Zimmer, "Could you please possibly call someone, or tell us who to call, to delay the destruction of the house slightly while we find out how valuable Harmony is?"

"I think the delay can be arranged," said Mr. Zimmer, smiling, as he pulled his phone from his pocket.

Mr. Zimmer was also the gardener for the mayor, and he called Mr. Barnard to tell him about the valuable find and to explain that the doll was thought to be worth a substantial sum. He then suggested that a delay of donating the contents of the house, along with its demolition, might be in order.

When he finished his conversation, with an even bigger smile on his face, Mr. Zimmer stowed his phone and told them, "Both the mayor and his wife will be here in about an hour. Mrs. Barnard sits on the Town Planning Committee," he added, "so I'm sure she will want to be a part of this too."

"That would give us time to look at the diaries again," said Kyle, looking sideways at Enilsa.

"Good idea," Enilsa replied.

Mr. Zimmer let them back into the house right away. After unpacking Harmony again, and carefully placing her on the dining table atop the spread-out quilt, they made their way upstairs to once more explore Laura's diaries.

Enilsa, scanning a few of the earliest entries in the first diary, was the first to find something relevant. "Laura and her mother took a trip to

New York City when she was eight," she said. Enilsa then proceeded to read the last paragraph of the entry.

"A nice man gave me something very special, and Mother said I could keep it. He said I reminded him of his little girl, who died, and he made the special gift as a tribute to her. He asked me to keep it a secret, and I promised. But he said I could tell David, so I did."

"So Laura probably looked like Harmony when she was young," said Roberta. "How cute."

"It's more likely the man was just so full of grief," Enilsa said, "that any blond girl reminded him of his daughter."

Kyle was the next to find something interesting related to the doll. "This is about ten years before the earthquake," he said.

"I just read an amazing article in The Herald. The special gift I got when I was eight and we went to New York is incredibly valuable! No one seems to know what happened to it, and people all over the world are looking for it. I had no idea! But I would never want to part with it, so it doesn't matter. I'm telling David about the article, but no one else."

After about twenty minutes more of reading, Cassie found something too. "This is just after the earthquake," she said, "and about a week after the entry we read with the green-blue-red clue."

"I am sending Mrs. Peters a lemon poppy seed cake. She alone is responsible for saving the treasure that I always kept in the upstairs sewing room. Evidently, when I broke my leg last year and Mrs. Peters came in for a month to do the cleaning, she moved the green trunk to the cupboard under the stairs. Thank goodness! And to think, I was so annoyed at her for rearranging everything in the kitchen to where I couldn't find anything. I am so thankful now that she was such an industrious reorganizer."

They didn't read any more entries because they could hear Mr. and Mrs. Barnard arriving downstairs.

Both the mayor and his wife were thrilled with the find.

"We have been searching for some way to save this house," said Mrs. Barnard.

"Yes," added the mayor. "We really wanted to do the Town History Museum as Laura wished. West Bend is well over a hundred years old. It's high time we had a museum to celebrate our history."

However, Mrs. Barnard cautioned them. "This might get tricky if anyone else tries to claim the doll; for example, if Mr. Brigita had any heirs."

Shaking their heads, Enilsa and Kyle both tried to speak at once. Kyle let Enilsa go first, and she rapidly said, "Laura's diary entries are proof that the doll was given to her. So it was her property."

"Exactly," said Kyle, who had been about to say the same thing. "She is the rightful owner of Harmony. I don't think there can be any doubt."

They were right. The documentation in Laura's diaries was enough proof that the doll was rightfully hers.

Next, Mrs. Barnard carefully examined the doll; and she seemed to be looking for something. Gingerly removing one of Harmony's shoes and slipping off her lacy sock, she stated, "There!" as she pointed. An old-fashioned scrolling signature was sprawled across the bottom of Harmony's left foot, and they could just make out the name of Monterrey Brigita. "To this day," said Mrs. Barnard, "many doll makers sign their dolls. And this can help prove its authenticity."

Though Cassie was happy that the house demolition was most likely permanently cancelled, she suddenly realized something. "We aren't going to be around to find out how this plays out," she told Enilsa.

"Oh, I totally forgot," responded Enilsa.

"We're going upstate next week to visit my cousin, Beatrice, at the Candlewick Inn," explained Cassie. "We'll be gone two weeks. This has been so exciting," she added, with disappointment in her voice, "I don't want to miss the rest of what's going to happen."

"If anything big develops while you're gone, we can call you," suggested Kyle. "Just leave us the number of the inn."

"Okay," said Enilsa. "That's a good plan."

"And if nothing big develops," said Roberta, "we'll just fill you in on the little stuff when you get back." The twins fully intended to follow the whole Harmony thing through; it was very exciting to be part of something so wonderful. And Roberta definitely planned to keep in touch with her new friends, even after everything was settled with the doll and the plans for the museum.

Next, in a dreamy voice, Roberta speculated, "I wonder if Harmony might be worth a million dollars."

The others, though hopeful, thought her speculation might be a little far-fetched.

As it turns out, Roberta didn't fetch nearly far enough because Harmony sold through a large auction house five weeks later for over three million dollars. By that time, Cassie and Enilsa had already solved another mystery at the

Candlewick Inn. So, all in all, they were having an incredibly thrilling summer.

The town of West Bend now had enough money to completely restore *Ninety-Seven Burleson Avenue*, which was soon to become the Town History Museum. There was also enough money to build a new library and purchase land along the river for a park to be called Lippincott Park.

Mr. Zimmer ended up moving six of the heirloom rosebushes back to the house. He left the rest in the town square for everyone to enjoy.

Shortly after Harmony was auctioned, the story was presented as front-page news in the local paper. The lengthy article featured the four young detectives, along with the details of how they had uncovered the mysterious treasure. Mr. Zimmer, Mrs. Brinkley, Mr. Duncan, and Mr. Haupt were also included in the story. And they all posed for a picture with Harmony before she left for her new home in Canada.

When the museum opened the next year, a copy of the article was framed and hung on the wall next to a display in the parlor that included the green trunk, David Lippincott's coins, the other toys, and Laura's diaries.

Also, a new custom-made transom was installed over the front door of the Town History Museum. Wanda Sloan donated the glass, which contained another special message:

~ This house was saved by Harmony ~

About the Author

J.H. Sweet lives in South Texas and has a degree in English from Texas State University. Ms. Sweet is the author of *The Fairy Chronicles*, *Foo and Friends*, *Juan Noel's Crystal Airship*, *Cassie Kingston Mysteries*, and *The Heaviest Things*.

jhsweet.com

Cassie Kingston Mysteries

Mysteries seem to be seeking out Cassie Kingston and her best friend, Enilsa Santos. Their adventures begin unexpectedly, and the pair end up solving four mysteries during one summer break. With help from several friends, Cassie and Enilsa outwit a clever forger, find real treasure, solve a mystery involving a bronze statue, save a house from being demolished, and uncover the truth about a strange painting of an island. *Chapter Books Ages 8+*

The Message in the Transom

While helping to transplant rosebushes, Cassie and Enilsa, along with two of their friends, begin to uncover secrets involving an old house. Following a series of clues that begins with a strange message in a stained-glass transom, the friends work to save the house from demolition. With both diligence and ingenuity, the new sleuths end up finding something so valuable, it can only be described as *A Treasure Beyond Measure.*

The Candlewick Inn Mystery

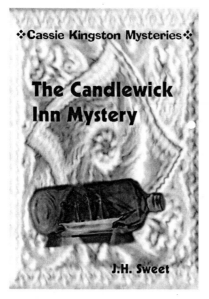

Surely, it can't be possible to find two treasures in one summer. But that's exactly what Cassie and Enilsa are trying to do. While spending two weeks helping out at the Candlewick Inn, a property Cassie's cousin will soon inherit from their late Great-Aunt Sybil, the girls find several clues relating to something valuable hidden at the inn. While investigating, they receive messages from a psychic, and even a note from Great-Aunt Sybil herself, which help them solve *The Candlewick Inn Mystery*.

The Statue in Glen Park

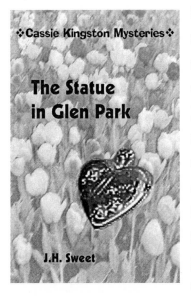

Upon returning from Glen Park, and looking at photographs from the outing, Cassie and Enilsa are shocked to discover that a serious crime was apparently committed right under their unsuspecting noses. But could this possibly be a classic case where the camera lens sees something very different than the human eye? However, as their investigation unfolds, an unexpected turn of events leads the girls to believe that a fanciful bronze statue may hold the real answer to the mystery.

The Painting of Swan Cove Island

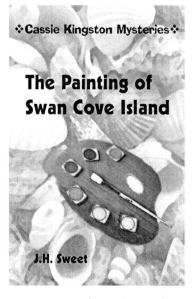

During a three-week vacation to visit Enilsa's grandmother on Swan Cove Island, Cassie and Enilsa discover an unusual painting that leads them on a pirate treasure hunt. However, they soon discover that appearances can be very deceiving and that real treasure is often found in the most unlikely places.

Also by J.H. Sweet

Foo and Friends

What are your lawn and garden ornaments up to when no one is looking? If they hold magical spirits like most gnomes, angels, gargoyles, and foo dogs, you can bet it's something pretty important. Join Foo and his Friends on some of their important adventures as they help keep our neighborhoods safe and in tip-top shape. *For read aloud and early chapter readers ages 6+.*

The Wishing Well

Magical foo dogs generally work in pairs to protect us from evil spirits. Unfortunately, Foo no longer has his partner because Foo-Too was taken away to the Resting Place of Retired Foos. Having to make it on his own is bad enough, but Foo also has to get used to living in a brand new neighborhood. Thank goodness he is meeting plenty of other magical lawn and garden ornaments who can help him figure things out.

The Garage Sale

Bad news has fallen on the neighborhood: Some of the Friends are going to be sold in a big garage sale. Foo Magic doesn't really work to solve problems like this, so a midnight meeting is definitely called for. But as the Friends work on a plan to save Henrietta (the plastic owl), will they also have time to save a turtle sandbox named Ruben? More panic erupts when Gilbert, the wire reindeer, also gets added to the list of For-Sale items. Can it be stopped, or is it meant to be? And will the neighborhood ever be the same again?

The Fake Foo

Foo dogs, gargoyles, garden angels, and gnomes all have the ability to protect people from harm, which is why Foo is so puzzled as to why his new neighbors would place useless, for-decoration-only statues outside their home. However, when several evil spirits invade the neighborhood, Foo must figure out a way to help the Fake Foo protect their house and the people inside.

The Porch Swing Ghost

As if having to drive away a persistent ghost over and over again isn't bad enough, Foo must also battle a Foo Cold during the Annual Fix-Up-the-Playground Project. Things go from bad to worse when a rash of burglaries, by a very crafty burglar, hits the neighborhood. With so much going on, will Foo be able to take care of business as usual? And will anyone be able to find out who is playing doorbell tricks?

Juan Noel's Crystal Airship
The Story of a
Christmas Eve Legend

On a magical six-hour Christmas Eve journey aboard the Crystal Airship, managed by Juan Noel, four children and various other passengers hopscotch the countries and continents of the world, making important deliveries to help keep hopes and dreams alive. *For all ages.*

Juan Noel's
Crystal Airship

J.H. Sweet

The Heaviest Things

How can we lift something extremely heavy when we can't see or touch the thing? In an effort to help an elderly neighbor, ten-year-old Henry Goodwin sets out to discover how some of the heaviest and most mysterious things on earth have been moved. His research yields surprising results when he meets a real-life Paul Bunyan, has a conversation with the god Atlas, and takes a trip to the North Pole. However, even after traveling far and wide, Henry discovers that the answer to his own problem lies much closer to home. *Chapter Book Ages 8+*

The
Heaviest
Things

J.H. Sweet

CPSIA information can be obtained at www.ICGtesting.com
Printed in the USA
LVOW08s2138180614

390731LV00001B/98/P